QUESTION IT!

WATER
IS THERE ENOUGH FOR EVERYONE?

PHILIP STEELE

WAYLAND

First published in Great Britain
in 2017 by Wayland
Copyright © Wayland, 2017
All rights reserved

Produced by Tall Tree Ltd
Editor: Jon Richards
Designer: Ed Simkins

ISBN: 978 1 5263 0214 4
10 9 8 7 6 5 4 3 2 1

MIX
Paper from
responsible source
FSC
www.fsc.org
FSC® C10474

Wayland
An imprint of Hachette
Children's Group
Part of Hodder and Stoughton
Carmelite House
50 Victoria Embankment
London EC4Y 0DZ

An Hachette UK Company
www.hachette.co.uk
www.hachettechildrens.co.uk

Printed and bound in China

CONTENTS

IT'S TIME TO TALK ABOUT
WATER

It has no colour. It has no smell. Even though we use water every day, we hardly give it a thought. Yet it is water that keeps us and our world alive. Without it we could not exist.

SHAPING OUR PLANET

Seen from space, our planet looks blue, with patches of white cloud. Salty oceans cover about 70 per cent of Earth's surface. Water has shaped our rocks, our valleys and hills, our coasts and soils over billions of years.

People struggle to travel through flooded streets in Thailand. Monsoon rains cause flooding in many parts of southern Asia every year.

'Water is good. It benefits all things...'

Laozi, Chinese philosopher, c.604–531 BCE

4

WATER IS LIFE

Life on Earth began in the water, sometime between 4.2 and 3.5 billion years ago. Then, some 445 million years ago, all sorts of life forms evolved in water and slowly began to move on to land.

Our climate on Earth is created by water and by the Sun. The amount of rainfall determines the plant and animal life in any one region. Water and climate influence every aspect of human life. They affect population numbers, where and how we live, our health, our farming and food, our energy and industry.

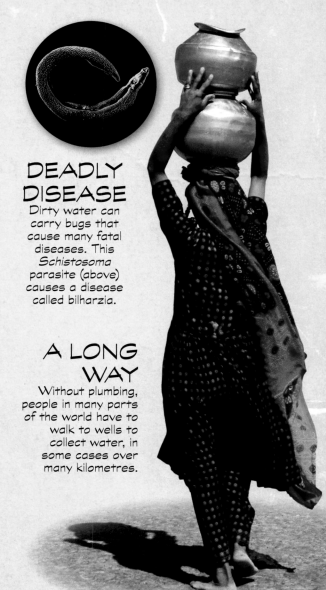

DEADLY DISEASE

Dirty water can carry bugs that cause many fatal diseases. This *Schistosoma* parasite (above) causes a disease called bilharzia.

A LONG WAY

Without plumbing, people in many parts of the world have to walk to wells to collect water, in some cases over many kilometres.

FLOODWATERS

A large proportion of the world's population lives on or close to the coast. Strong rains and tides can cause devastating floods.

HYDROELECTRICITY

Flowing water has been used for thousands of years to power mills and factories. Today, we build huge dams, such as the Pak Mun Dam in Thailand (above), which convert the flow of water to produce electricity.

The world's climate is changing. The amount of water we use is changing and the population is growing. In each chapter of this book we'll look at different aspects of the topic of water, exploring and discussing the issues involved. There are vital questions to be raised and discussed.

Let's talk about them.

SO, WHAT IS WATER?

The chemical formula is H_2O. This means that each molecule of water binds one oxygen atom together with two hydrogen atoms. Water exists as a liquid, but also as a solid (ice) and as a gas (water vapour). Many minerals and other substances dissolve in water, such as the salts found in seawater. Water with a very low level of salts or other dissolved solids is called fresh water. We use fresh water for drinking, washing, cooking and watering plants.

FRESH WATER SOURCES

Fresh water makes up less than 3 per cent of all the water on our planet. Much of that is deep frozen all year round in the ice caps surrounding the North and South Poles. We can only access a tiny amount of fresh water, less than 0.01 per cent of the total, from lakes and rivers. More fresh water can be found underground.

0.01% accessible

3% fresh water

97% salt water

WHY DO WE NEED IT?

Humans need to drink water to stay alive. A healthy adult living in a mild climate needs at least 1.5 litres during the course of a day. Our blood and our body tissues contain water and water forms part of the body's natural chemical processes, such as digesting food. Water brings nutrients from food to our body cells, while urine carries away unwanted waste. Water helps to regulate our body temperature, for example when we sweat. It also protects parts of the body from knocks and helps our joints to move smoothly.

Up to 65%

90%

NUMBER CRUNCH

50 to 65 per cent of an adult's body is made up of water. Our brains are about 90 per cent water!

THE WATER CYCLE

Water is finite. There is only so much of it to go round, and we cannot make any more of it. The water on the planet is in endless motion, part of a cycle created by the warmth of the Sun.

HOW DOES THE WATER CYCLE WORK?

3 As the water vapour rises, it cools. This turns it back into tiny droplets of liquid water, which form clouds, fog or mist in the air.

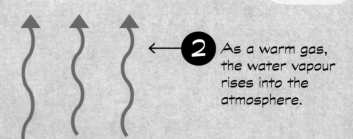

2 As a warm gas, the water vapour rises into the atmosphere.

THREE STATES
The temperature range on Earth means that water can exist in its three states — liquid water, solid ice and gassy water vapour.

1 The liquid water on the Earth's surface evaporates or turns into vapour when heated by the Sun.

In the sea, the water evaporates and the cycle begins all over again.

FOR GOOD OR FOR BAD

Human progress has always depended on the water cycle, but it has often cost us dearly. For thousands of years people have settled near rivers, where there is plenty of water for drinking and irrigating crops. Along the banks of the Yellow River in China, flooding left behind a rich muddy soil where crops would grow well. However, over the ages the same floods have also killed many millions of people. Humans have always battled to control and manage water as well as use it.

 As droplets collect together, they become heavy. They fall to the ground as rain, or in frozen forms such as hail, snow or sleet. This is called precipitation.

5 In some places, the rainwater collects to form lakes or underground water stores.

 The rainwater may bubble up as springs. Rain may also run off directly into streams and rivers, and flow down to the sea.

> 'Water is the driving force of all nature.'
>
> Leonardo da Vinci, Italian artist, sculptor, inventor and engineer, 1452–1519

TURN ON THE TAP

Water needs to be collected and stored. On a small scale, rainwater may be collected in butts, cisterns or tanks and used by a single household or a village. Modern towns and cities in the developed world are served by huge reservoirs. These can be formed by rivers or lakes that have been dammed to collect the water.

The Hoover Dam lies between the US states of Nevada and Arizona. It holds back the waters of Lake Mead, the largest reservoir by volume in the US.

CLEANING WATER

Reservoir water must be processed at a special plant before it can be used. Particles in the water settle and any twigs or leaves are screened out. The water is then filtered through layers of coarse and fine sand. Chemicals such as chlorine or hypochlorites are added to kill off any bacteria and other microbes that could make people ill.

PIPED TO THE HOME

The water is then piped and pumped along water mains to each building. Here it may be used in central heating radiators or released through hot or cold taps for use in bathrooms, kitchens or washing machines. Few things have changed people's everyday lives as much as easy access to water.

EASY ACCESS

Many wealthy countries can afford to build large and complicated systems that deliver water right into your home when you turn on a tap.

LET'S DISCUSS...
MAINS WATER

UK

Average consumption per person per day (litres)

Recommended (UN figures)

160

Africa 20

50

• is clean and good for public health.

• is convenient and accessible.

• can be recycled and used again.

• encourages people to use much more water than they need.

• needs expensive maintenance and repair.

• is not available in many parts of the world.

WATER FROM THE WELL

In the more developed parts of the world, about 87 per cent of people can get clean, treated water straight from the bathroom tap. But elsewhere it's a different story. One third of the world's population – that's about 2.5 billion people – have no water piped to their homes.

NATURAL SOURCES

Instead, they have to fetch their water from natural sources, such as springs, rivers or wells. Dig deep into the ground in many places and you will probably reach some water. Even under the world's largest hot desert, the Sahara, there are underground reserves of water.

This oasis, surrounded by sand dunes, lies in the Ica region of southern Peru, close to the Pacific Ocean.

GROUND WATER

Rocks, gravel and sand that soak up or trap rainwater underground are called aquifers. The level to which the ground is saturated is called the water table. Digging a deep well by hand can be dangerous. Modern drilling is much safer, but expensive. Engineers drill down to reach the aquifer. If the water is under pressure from the surrounding rocks it may rise to the surface naturally. If not, it will need a pump.

A LONG WALK

Wells are often far from a village, and people have to walk for hours each day carrying heavy containers of water. It is tiring and takes up time that could be spent at school or farming the land. One clever invention has been the plastic water drum, which can be pulled along the ground. People in dry and remote areas need new wells, but there may not be enough water to go round. The supply needs to be sustainable.

FETCH AND CARRY

These women are collecting water from a well in the Indian town of Vasai, close to Mumbai, India.

In Africa, only 4 per cent of available water resources can be accessed, because of the lack of wells, pipes, pumps and reservoirs.

4%

| 1 litre | 1 litre | 1 litre | 1 litre | 1 litre |
| 1 litre | 1 litre | 1 litre | 1 litre | 1 litre |

In some developing countries, each person on average uses only 10 litres of water a day (see page 11).

LET'S DISCUSS...
WATER FROM WELLS

• keeps people alive in remote areas.

• allows people to water their crops.

• can now be pumped using solar power.

• will run dry when the aquifer is used up.

• has to be fetched and carried.

• may become contaminated or dirty.

WATER
FROM THE SEA

If we could drink the water from the ocean, we could solve all our water shortages. But we can't, at least not very easily. Seawater is salty and drinking it makes us ill. Some inland water in rivers and lakes is also a bit too salty, or brackish. Salt water is not good for irrigation either, as it destroys crops.

FILTERING

Taking the salt out of seawater is called desalination. Various industrial processes can be used. One method is called reverse osmosis. This screens and filters the seawater and then pumps it through spiral membranes under very high pressure. Typically, every two litres of seawater can produce one litre of fresh water.

REVERSE OSMOSIS
These tubes are using special sheets, or membranes, to remove tiny particles from water using reverse osmosis, making it suitable for drinking.

DESALINATION

In recent years, the technology used for large-scale desalination has become a lot smarter. Desalination is now being used in 120 countries, including Saudi Arabia and Spain. This way of accessing water is likely to grow in the future in regions where there is little rainfall and a high risk of drought.

On a small scale, pots or even home-made desalination kits can be used to produce water for a single household. Water in a container is heated or warmed by the sun. The liquid water turns into vapour, leaving behind salts and any other particles. The vapour passes through a tube into a cool container, where it condenses into drinkable water. This process is called distilling.

This large-scale desalination plant lies on the coast of the Spanish island of Lanzarote in the Atlantic Ocean.

In every kilogram of seawater there are 35 grams of dissolved salts.

LET'S DISCUSS...
LARGE-SCALE DESALINATION

- accesses the world's biggest source of water.
- saves using up existing fresh water sources.
- uses much improved technology.

- has to be located on coasts or islands.
- is expensive to install.
- leaves behind highly concentrated brine and other contaminants.

ENDING POVERTY

According to the United Nations, by 2025, 1.8 billion people in the world will be living in regions where there will be a severe shortage of water. Who will be hardest hit? The world's poorest countries.

A boy collects dirty water from a well in the village of Mpaana in Uganda, Africa.

QUESTION IT!
IS ACCESSING WATER THE BEST WAY TO END POVERTY?

WITHOUT GOOD ACCESS TO WATER it is hard to organise farming, healthcare, education or new industries. Water poverty means economic poverty.

WATER IS NOT DISTRIBUTED in even quantities around the world. Sixty per cent of the world's people who live in lands that are short of water are unable to grow enough crops for their food.

POOR FARMERS OR HERDERS CANNOT AFFORD TO DRILL and maintain new wells. That is why many international organisations fund the building of new wells in regions at risk from drought.

NEW WELLS MAY NOT ALWAYS BE THE ANSWER. They may be hard or too expensive to maintain. They may take too much water from aquifers. They may encourage people to live in places that are not sustainable in the long term, and so prolong poverty.

WATER SHORTAGE IS JUST ONE OF MANY REASONS FOR POVERTY. Unfair trade agreements, corruption, bad government and warfare all prevent development. The wider political problems also need sorting out in order to defeat poverty.

17

2 THE HEAT IS ON

Weather is what we experience every day, come rain or shine. Climate is the pattern of weather in any given place over a longer period, perhaps 30 years or more. Water plays a key role in the global climate system.

This painting shows people skating on the frozen canals of Rotterdam, the Netherlands, in 1825. It is thought that winters were more severe at that time.

COOLING AND WARMING

Of course the climate can change. It always has done. In the past, Earth has been gripped by ice ages, and has warmed during the periods in between, known as interglacials. At the moment Earth should be cooling, but it's not. It's cooking. World temperatures began to rise during the factory age of the 1800s, and they are now soaring. Is that due to a natural variability in our climate? More than 97 per cent of scientists think not. They argue that climate change has been created by human activities.

CAUSING THE 'GREENHOUSE' EFFECT

Many people blame gases such as carbon dioxide (CO_2). These are pumped out into the atmosphere by factory chimneys, forest fires, planes, cars and construction sites. They collect in the atmosphere. As heat from the Sun is reflected back from Earth's surface, it is trapped by these greenhouse gases and bounced back again. This reflected heat warms the atmosphere even more, disrupting weather patterns and melting ice caps.

GREENHOUSE GASES
Many people believe that polluting gases from car exhausts and factories are responsible for increasing the greenhouse effect.

NUMBER CRUNCH
The surface temperature of Earth's land and oceans has risen by between 0.65 and 1.06°C since 1880.

LET'S DISCUSS...
CARBON DIOXIDE

- is part of the natural cycle of life on Earth.
- is absorbed by the oceans in large quantities.
- is absorbed by the world's great rainforests.

- is one of the gases overheating our planet.
- is making the oceans more acidic.
- is increasing as the world's forests are being destroyed.

WILD WATER, DRY LAND

Human activities have often created problems with water in the past. Overgrazing or intensive farming sometimes destroy the vegetation and roots that trap moisture in the soil, turning land into desert or a dust bowl. If people cut down trees in river valleys, the soil erodes, and this can cause disastrous flooding downstream.

DROUGHT AND FLOODS

Scientists predict that human-made climate change will bring a new age of drought, floods and extreme storms. Indeed, it is already happening. In a warmer world, the air heats up and expands, and it can hold more water vapour for rain. The effects of climate change are hard to predict. Different regions may be affected in very different ways, or suffer more because of natural variations. These include the El Niño climate cycle in the Pacific, which causes extreme flooding and drought on opposite sides of the planet.

Prolonged dry periods, known as droughts, cause the ground to dry out and crack, and crops cannot grow in it.

WILD WEATHER
As more and more energy is released into the atmosphere, we may see an increase in severe weather events, such as hurricanes.

CHANGING PATTERNS

In places that have often had droughts in the past, the periods of intense heat without rain are becoming longer and more extreme. The old climate patterns have changed, so nobody is sure when to plant crops any more. Even when the rains do come, they may flood the hard, baked soil. Have humans turned water, their best friend, into their own worst enemy?

EXTREME DROUGHT

Animal bones litter the ground in the Kruger National Park, South Africa. Prolonged drought threatens water supplies for people and animals.

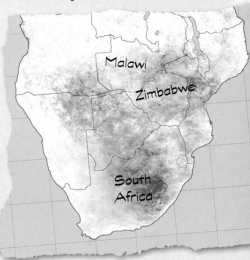

NUMBER CRUNCH

A long drought in southern Africa, associated with El Niño, is threatening food supplies and public health. The map on the right shows how temperatures have increased between 2000 and 2015. The red areas represent areas that were hotter than usual during this period. By 2016, about 14 million people were being affected in countries such as Malawi, Zimbabwe and South Africa.

THINK ABOUT...
CLIMATE CHANGE

- increases water shortages in many regions.
- increases the danger of flooding in others.
- makes extreme storms more likely.

TROUBLE AT SEA

The oceans are the great engines of our climate. Currents of cold or warm water circulate between the Equator and the Poles. One of them, called the North Atlantic Drift, warms the shores of northwest Europe and gives the region a mild climate. Seasonal monsoons carry water from the Indian Ocean to fall in torrents of rain on the parched lands of southern Asia.

With less sea ice to hunt on in the Arctic, polar bears find it harder to catch food, and have to travel farther and farther to get enough to survive.

Arctic Ocean

Atlantic Ocean

Pacific Ocean

Pacific Ocean

Indian Ocean

Southern Ocean

SWIRLING CURRENTS

This map shows the main ocean currents carrying warm (red) and cold (blue) water around the globe.

SEA CHANGE

When it comes to global warming, the oceans do us a favour, because they naturally absorb a lot of the problematic carbon dioxide. The trouble is, the CO_2 levels in the ocean are now so high that they are making the seawater acidic. This damages all sorts of marine habitats, such as coral reefs. The oceans also expand as they warm. This makes sea levels rise, so that they flood lowlands and islands. On coral islands in the Pacific Ocean, rising saltwater can soak into freshwater aquifers, making wells unusable.

NUMBER CRUNCH

About 23 per cent of the world's population lives on or near the coast. Sea level rises will present a huge problem.

ARCTIC MELT

Sea levels also rise because much of the polar ice is melting. The Arctic sea ice has shrunk by 20 per cent since 1979. Part of the East Antarctic ice sheet has actually been growing, probably because of a natural current switch in the Pacific Ocean. Sea levels are expected to carry on rising for a long time, even if we cut down on CO_2 emissions now.

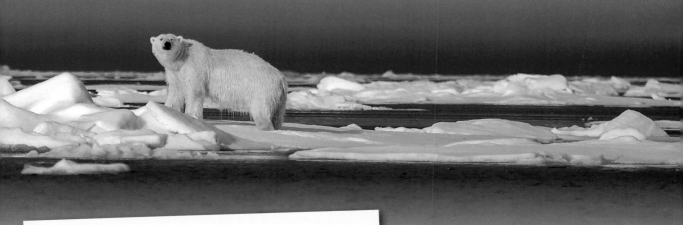

FLOOD DEFENCES

These flood defences in the Netherlands are designed to hold back rising sea levels. However, they are expensive to construct and not every country can afford to build them.

THINK ABOUT...
THE ARCTIC

• The tundra is melting, releasing more greenhouse gases.

• More shipping as sea ice melts means even more carbon emissions.

• Melting ice is raising sea levels.

TACKLING CLIMATE CHANGE

In 1992, the United Nations held the first Earth Summit in Rio de Janeiro, Brazil. Since then, policies have been agreed to deal with water shortage, storms and floods caused by or made worse by climate change. But are they going to work?

QUESTION IT!

ARE WE DOING ENOUGH TO TACKLE CLIMATE CHANGE?

THE PARIS SUMMIT IN 2015 set a target of limiting the increase in global warming to under 2°C. Some scientists predict that this could result in zero carbon emissions by the middle of this century.

GREEN MEASURES include planting new forests to soak up more carbon dioxide, and preventing forests being cut down. In recent decades, forests have absorbed 30 per cent of global CO_2 emissions.

NUMBER CRUNCH

Water shortages, made worse by climate change, could reduce the ability of countries to create wealth – their gross domestic product or GDP – by 6 per cent.

ECONOMIC MEASURES include taxes on fossil fuels or trade-offs in carbon quotas between nations. Countries are told how much carbon they can produce. If they wish to go above this set limit, they must purchase allowances from another country's quotas.

'... any further temperature increase will spell the total demise of Tuvalu... Surely, we must aim for the best future we can deliver and not a weak compromise.'

Enele Sopoaga, Prime Minister of the Pacific island state of Tuvalu, 2015

MOST SCIENTISTS AGREE ABOUT THE EFFECTS of climate change, but policy-making is in the hands of future politicians, who might disagree or not want to take serious action.

TARGETS NEED TO BE ENFORCED. Illegal logging and mining are still big problems. About 30 per cent of logging is illegal. In South America and Southeast Asia up to 80 per cent is illegal, much of it carried out by criminal organisations.

WATER AND HEALTH

We all think of water as something clean that keeps us alive. But for many people in the world, water is unhealthy and even a threat to life itself. About 3.5 million people are thought to die each year from diseases caused by drinking, washing or cooking with contaminated water.

IS IT SAFE?
In some parts of the world, the same source of water is used for cleaning, washing, drinking, cooking and even as a toilet.

POOR ACCESS

About 2.5 billion people in the world have no access to proper toilets or drainage. They mostly live in remote country areas, or in city slums. Human or animal waste may seep into rivers or ground water, and contaminate wells. A supply of safe, clean water is one of the greatest needs around the world.

About 783 million people in the world do not have access to clean water – that's more than one in ten.

NUMBER CRUNCH

These children in the Indian city of Mumbai are learning how washing and personal hygiene help to prevent the spread of diseases.

WATER-BORNE DISEASES

Water may be the breeding ground for insects such as mosquito larvae. A parasite from some mosquito species spreads deadly malaria, which killed about 438,000 people in 2015. Other diseases carried by water include cholera and dysentery. These were once common in cities such as London and Paris, until proper sewers and water works were constructed in the 1860s. Sanitation is essential for public health. Money is also well spent on education – teaching children the importance of washing their hands or boiling water to make it safe.

LET'S DISCUSS...
CLEAN WATER SUPPLIES

- are being installed in many parts of the world.
- prevent all sorts of diseases.
- save money on hospitals and healthcare.

- are still not available to millions of people.
- are expensive to install.
- must be protected against pollution.

27

POLLUTION PERIL

All sorts of industrial chemicals, detergents, pesticides, metals and household garbage find their way into lakes, rivers and oceans. They pollute the water and threaten the health of plants, animals and humans.

RIVERS THAT DIED

Rain washes nitrogen from fertilisers used on farmland into rivers and estuaries such as the Mississippi Delta. This reduces the levels of oxygen that support life, so a whole food chain is soon destroyed and huge areas become 'dead zones'. In the 1960s, the Cuyahoga River, in Ohio, USA, became so polluted that it caught fire. New clean river laws were passed there and in many other countries, but they are not always enforced. One of the most polluted rivers is the Citarum, in Java, Indonesia, which is massively poisoned with lead.

Rubbish and waste clogs up a river in the southern Indian state of Tamil-Nadu.

'We know that when we protect our oceans we're protecting our future.'

Bill Clinton, 42nd US President

THE TOXIC OCEANS

The pollution of the oceans can be just as bad. A spill from the *Deepwater Horizon* oil rig in the Gulf of Mexico in 2010 released 4.6 million barrels of sticky black oil into the sea. It killed fish and birds, affected the tourism and fishing industries and exposed humans to toxins. A major disaster at the Fukushima Daiichi nuclear complex in Japan poured radioactive water into the Pacific Ocean in 2011, and is still doing so more than five years later.

RAGING FIRE
The fire on the *Deepwater Horizon* led to the largest oil spill is US waters.

MICROPLASTICS
Microplastics, such as these fibres, are tiny pieces of plastic that are smaller than 1 mm. They are used in a wide range of products, such as cosmetics, and enter the environment during industrial processes or when we wash.

The world's oceans are filling up with plastic. As well as debris, there are tiny particles of industrial plastic. In the Pacific Ocean, these have formed a gigantic floating garbage patch. They are swallowed by fish and marine mammals. Polluting water means poisoning the planet's life-support system.

LET'S DISCUSS...
TACKLING POLLUTION

- New laws have cleaned up cities.
- Fish soon return to rivers that have been cleaned up.
- International laws now prevent dumping at sea.

- Clearing up an oil spill can cost billions of pounds.
- Oil companies still want to drill in the Arctic Ocean.
- Noise made by humans and machines can also harm marine creatures.

RAINFORESTS THREATENED

The Amazon drains about 7,050,000 square km of tropical land and pours 209 million litres of water into the Atlantic Ocean every second. The Amazon's rainforest has been under attack from illegal loggers and ranchers. In places, miners have poisoned its precious water.

QUESTION IT!
SHOULD WE BLAME ILLEGAL GOLD MINERS FOR POISONING THE AMAZON?

SOME 30,000 MINERS FIRST CAME TO THE PERUVIAN part of the forest in the 1980s, to pan the rivers.

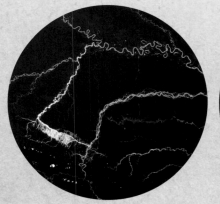 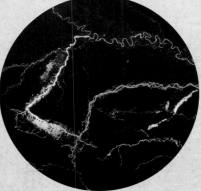

NUMBER CRUNCH

The Amazon delivers about 25 per cent of all the fresh water flowing into the oceans.

BEFORE AND AFTER

These two satellite images taken in 2003 (left) and 2011 (right) show the effects of gold mining in the Peruvian Amazon forest. The lighter areas show how 5,060 hectares of forest were cleared by the actions of miners during this time.

GANGS OF MINERS TURNED UP IN THE 1990S. They used highly toxic mercury to flush out the gold. Today, about 50,000 hectares of rainforest and river have been devastated.

THE MERCURY POISONED THE FISH that local people ate. It contaminated the river, the air and the soil. The toxic water poisoned the people.

THE MINERS WERE JUST PART OF A MUCH BIGGER PICTURE across the region. Ranchers cleared and burned forest in Brazil, and were ready to kill indigenous people or campaigners who got in their way.

IT WAS THE MINERS WHO POISONED THE RIVERS IN PERU. But they were desperately poor, and could not afford to decontaminate the region when their work was done.

FARMING AND CROPS

Water is vital for growing the food that we need to stay alive. Some crops are watered naturally, by rainfall, flooding or a wetland habitat. Others need watering by channels, sprays or pipes. Some crops are very 'thirsty', especially wheat, sugarcane and cotton. Some types of rice need to grow in deep flooded fields, others in shallow fields or irrigated terraces.

IRRIGATION PROBLEMS

Irrigation can be wasteful as water evaporates and pipes may leak. Too much irrigation makes the water table rise. This sometimes dissolves salty minerals in the soil, which then form a crust on the surface. Too much water extraction for irrigation can also lead to disaster. The Aral Sea, once the fourth largest lake in the world, almost disappeared when water was taken to irrigate cotton fields in Central Asia. That may have been good for farmers, but was terrible news for fishermen and lakeside communities, who found themselves living in a desert.

WATER IN THE DESERT

Artificial irrigation systems have turned normally arid regions, such as parts of California, USA (left), into fertile farmland, but they require a lot of water.

THIRSTY PRODUCE

Cows and other farm animals need a lot of water to drink and to water the food crops they eat as well.

NUMBER CRUNCH

Farmers use about 69 per cent of all the accessible fresh water in the world.

Abandoned fishing vessels lie beached far from the receding waters of the Aral Sea.

LET'S DISCUSS...
FARM ANIMALS

- number about 20 billion worldwide.

- need water and fodder grown as crops.

- provide us with food, wool and other produce.

- take about 6,800 litres of water to produce 0.5 kg of beef.

- provide less value for money than cereal or vegetable crops.

- use pasture that could be used to grow crops.

CITIES AND INDUSTRIES

About 8 per cent of fresh water is used in towns and cities, for housing, offices, restaurants, public services, sanitation and swimming pools. However, some cities are built in the most unsuitable places, and face a future of severe water shortages.

The city of Las Vegas uses huge amounts of water, sometimes just to entertain, in what is a very dry region.

WHO GETS THE WATER?

In the USA, the city of Las Vegas uses up to 629 litres of water per person per day. It has a soaring population, but is built in an arid zone. Its main reservoir, Lake Mead on the dammed Colorado River, runs very low.

The city of Adelaide in South Australia depends for its water on the Murray–Darling river system. Water is extracted for many reasons, so in times of drought there is a risk of the city running dry. The question is, who should have priority – the city dwellers, or the farms and vineyards further upstream?

LOW WATERS
The white band around the banks of Lake Mead shows just how low the waters in the reservoir have sunk as demand increases but rainfall declines.

Not only can paper production use a lot of water, but paper mills can also produce a large amount of water pollution from organic particles and artificial chemicals.

MILLS AND MINES

About 23 per cent of fresh water is swallowed up by industries such as mining, metals, chemicals and petrochemicals. It may be used for cooling, diluting, dissolving, steaming, cleaning or processing. In the computer industry, very pure water is needed in the manufacture of silicon chips. It is important not to waste water. Drought is bad news for factories as well as for farms.

LET'S DISCUSS... THE TOURISM INDUSTRY

- attracts people to sunny parts of the world.
- boosts the local economy and provides employment.
- digs new boreholes for water supply.

- uses huge amounts of water often in areas of shortage or drought.
- pollutes and disturbs marine environments.
- contributes to global warming through increased travel.

HYDRO POWER

Water has been put to work by humans ever since the water wheel was invented over 2,000 years ago. In modern thermo-electric power stations, water is used as steam to drive the turbines, and also as a coolant. In hydroelectric schemes, the force of the water itself drives the turbines that generate the electricity.

The huge Three Gorges Dam in China was opened in 2003. Some people believe that the mass of water it creates has triggered earthquakes in the area.

DAMS AND TURBINES

Hydroelectric power is the most widely used of the renewable energy sources, providing 16 per cent of the world's electricity. It is planned to double the output by 2050, as this process releases no greenhouse gases. Hydroelectric turbines are often housed in big dams and operate when water from the reservoir is released. The Three Gorges Dam on China's Yangtze River contains 32 giant turbines to generate power. This dam also aims to reduce flooding downstream. Massive concrete dams do present problems. The building of the Three Gorges Dam forced 1.3 million people from their homes, flooded important archaeological sites, increased the risk of landslides and damaged the environment.

SMALL-SCALE POWER

This image shows a small-scale hydroelectric generator used to produce power for a village in northern Vietnam.

TIDAL AND WAVE POWER

Bridges or coastal barrages may also house turbines that are driven by the daily surges of the tide. All sorts of clever machines and buoys have also been invented called wave-energy converters (WECs). They make use of the motion of the waves to generate electricity. Wave power is not yet widely used, but it shows promise for the future.

WAVE POWER
The Pelamis Wave Energy Converter is a large, snake-like device that uses the up-and-down motion of sea waves to produce electricity.

LET'S DISCUSS...
HYDROELECTRIC POWER

• is a sustainable source of power.

• is clean and does not emit greenhouse gases once built.

• can be generated on a large or a small scale.

• often relies on huge dams, which disrupt the environment.

• uses a lot of carbon-intensive concrete in dam construction.

• disrupts other economic uses of the river.

USING IT WISELY

Planet Earth is a giant machine for recycling water naturally. Because of climate change, pollution and drought, this system is in danger of breaking down. What can we do about this as individuals? We can campaign for clean water or protest against oil spills. But we can also do a lot in our daily lives to avoid wasting water.

QUESTION IT!
DO WE USE WATER WISELY IN THE HOME?

MANY BATHROOMS are now fitted with efficient showers that use about seven litres of water per minute instead of 20. Better working showers mean fewer CO_2 emissions from the boiler and less waste down the drain.

WASHING MACHINES are now fitted with many more settings than before, such as 'economy wash', which saves a huge amount of water. So too with dishwashers. If you wash up in a sink, don't leave the tap running while you rinse, use a plug.

FITTING A HALF-FLUSH OPTION FOR YOUR TOILET OR reducing the full flush could save your family 60,000 litres of water during a year.

14,000,000

NUMBER CRUNCH

It has been estimated that, in the UK, water equivalent to 14 million baths is lost daily because of leaking pipes and burst water mains.

THE LATEST SHOWERS, washing machines and dishwashers are expensive to buy. Many of us have old models that are not as efficient.

WATER USE IN THE HOME
These figures show how water is used in the average home of a wealthy country.

12.2% hand basin

21.8% flushing toilet

11.7% washing clothes

11.4% other

8.3% washing dishes

5.6% gardening

3.6% cooking and drinking

25.4% bath and shower

WATER IS ALL TOO EASY TO WASTE, AND WE ALL DO IT sometimes. We may use the dishwasher when it is only half-loaded, or boil a full kettle when we only need one that's half full, or have a bath instead of a shower.

WHO OWNS WATER?

The question of who owns water has been important throughout history. It is a key issue in dry lands, where water may be a question of survival. Thirst may drive people to conflict, but it may also force them to cooperate and share.

WATER LAWS

As far as the law in many countries is concerned, the people who own the land around the water are often considered the owners. They have what are called 'riparian' ('river bank') rights and can therefore access and use the water. In other places, the community or the state owns the water and issues permits to those who are entitled to access or use the water.

In some parts of the world, ownership of the land bordering a river gives you ownership of the river itself.

WATER PROTEST
In 2005, in the Bolivian city of El Alto, local residents protested against the foreign companies that owned their water supplier.

PRIVATE OR PUBLIC?

The supply of water may be run as a public service or by a private company. Private supply has often been challenged in less-developed countries. The companies say they are helping ordinary people gain access to a good water system. Protesters say the companies are making a profit from supplying people with what they need simply to stay alive. They say water should not be seen as a commodity like oil or timber. In Bolivia, the privatisation of water led to an increase in poverty. As a result, there were popular uprisings and protests, which led to water being returned to public ownership.

LET'S DISCUSS...
PRIVATE WATER COMPANIES

- have a powerful monopoly of supply and no competition.
- tend to put profits before people.
- may have conflicting commercial interests.

- claim to be better priced than the state.
- unlike most governments, can think beyond the next election.
- have specialist experience in many countries.

WATER IS A HUMAN RIGHT

Remember that in some parts of the world, clean, safe water is just not available – even out of a tap. Supplying water to all those who are in dire need should be a global priority, as should avoiding waste. Defining water access as an essential right makes that very clear.

QUESTION IT!
SHOULD WATER BE TREATED LIKE ANY OTHER COMMODITY?

IN 2010, THE UN DEFINED THE RIGHT TO water as the right of everyone to sufficient, safe, acceptable and physically accessible and affordable water for personal and domestic uses.

WATER RIGHTS
This poster was created by a European organisation that campaigns for worldwide clean drinking water and sanitation.

WATER is a Human Right

AS WITH OXYGEN, WATER is something we all need in order to stay alive, to remain healthy and to prosper. For all these reasons, the right to water has to be seen as an important and universal human right.

'The human right to water is indispensable for leading a life in human dignity. It is a prerequisite for the realisation of other human rights.'

United Nations resolution, 2010

A UNIVERSAL HUMAN RIGHT IS ONE OF THE BASIC NEEDS that everybody in the world requires in order to live a decent life.

DOESN'T IT MAKE SENSE TO TREAT WATER like any other commodity that can be bought and sold, rather than as a human right?

IF WATER IS NOT JUST A COMMODITY, why did Americans buy 1.7 billion half-litre plastic bottles of water every week in 2015, instead of turning on the tap?

THE FUTURE OF WATER

In the year 1800, the world was inhabited by about one billion people. Two hundred years later the world population had reached six billion. Today it is 7.5 billion and rising. Ten billion is predicted by 2083. The population clock is racing forwards at the same time as the climate change clock. It is a dangerous combination.

The cramped tower blocks of the city of Hong Kong show how human population pressures can dramatically increase the demand for water in a small area.

PEOPLE ON THE MOVE

Another process already under way is urbanisation. For many years, people around the world have been moving from the countryside into the towns and cities. At the same time in Asia and North Africa, war, natural disasters and poverty are forcing people to flee from their homes as refugees.

THINK WATER

Right now water has to be placed at the centre of our planning for the future. It affects both global and local economies, our cities, public health and the environment. We need to plan for water shortages, floods and rising sea levels, because if we do not manage water, it will manage us. If we can save water, however, we can save ourselves.

NUMBER CRUNCH

In 1800, the planet's population numbered one billion. This has soared to 7.5 billion today and is predicted to be ten billion by 2083.

1800   2016   2083

GLOSSARY

AQUIFER
Rock, gravel or sand that soak up or trap rainwater.

ARID ZONE
A region, like the desert around Las Vegas, where the climate is dry and there is very little fresh water available.

ATMOSPHERE
The air in any particular place or the gases surrounding Earth.

ATOM
The smallest particle of a chemical element that can exist.

BACTERIA
A large group of microorganisms, some of which can cause disease and, if found in water, can make people ill.

BASIN
An area of land that drains into a river or a container that holds water.

BRACKISH WATER
Also known as briny water, brackish water contains more salt than fresh water but not as much as seawater.

BRINE
Water that contains high levels of salt.

CARBON EMISSIONS
The release of carbon dioxide into the atmosphere. Human activities, such as burning oil, coal and gas and cutting down forests, have led to increased levels of carbon dioxide in the atmosphere.

CISTERN
A waterproof container that holds water, often used to collect rainwater.

CLIMATE
The weather conditions in an area over a long period.

COMMODITY
Something that can be bought or sold.

CONTAMINANT
A substance that pollutes water, making it unsuitable for use or for drinking.

DESALINATION
The removal of salt from water. Various industrial processes are used to remove salt from seawater.

DROUGHT
A period of below-average rain that leads to a shortage of water. It can last for days, months or even years.

DUST BOWL
An area of land where vegetation has been lost and soil reduced to dust, especially as a result of drought or unsuitable farming practices.

EVAPORATE
Turn from liquid into a vapour.

FINITE
Having a limit or an end. Water is finite because there is only so much available.

FOOD CHAIN
A series of plants and animals that are linked because each consumes the one below it in the chain.

FRESH WATER
Naturally occurring water, such as that found in glaciers, rivers and lakes, that is not salty and is not seawater.

GREENHOUSE GASES
Gases in the air that trap energy from the Sun and warm the Earth's surface and air. The most common greenhouse gases are water vapour, carbon dioxide and methane.

HYDROELECTRICITY
The generation of electricity by flowing water, the force of which drives a turbine.

ICE AGE
A time in the past when temperatures were very cold and glaciers covered large parts of the world.

INDIGENOUS
Naturally existing in a place or country rather than arriving from another place.

INTENSIVE FARMING
A way of farming and producing large amounts of crops by using chemicals and machines.

IRRIGATION
The supply of water to land so that crops and plants can grow.

MICROBE
A very small living thing, especially one that causes disease, that can only be seen with a microscope.

NUTRIENTS
Any substance that plants or animals need to live and grow. Drinking water helps to carry nutrients from food to body cells.

PETROCHEMICAL
Any chemical substance obtained from petroleum or natural gas.

PRECIPITATION
Water that falls from clouds as rain or in frozen form, such as hail, snow or sleet.

RENEWABLE ENERGY
Energy that is produced from ongoing sustainable resources, like wind, water or sunlight, rather than finite sources, such as oil or coal.

RESERVOIR
A large natural or man-made lake used as a source for water.

RIPARIAN
Relating to the banks of a river. People who own land around water and have riparian rights have the right to use and access the water.

SANITATION
Conditions essential for public health, especially the provision of clean drinking water and adequate sewage disposal.

SATURATED
Holding as much water or moisture as can be absorbed.

SEWER
An underground channel or pipe that carries away drainage water or waste material.

SUSTAINABLE
Able to be supplied and maintained at a certain level. Water supply needs to be sustainable.

THERMO-ELECTRIC
Producing electricity using different temperatures. In modern thermo-electric power stations water is used as steam to drive the turbines and also used as a coolant.

TUNDRA
A vast, flat, treeless Arctic region where the subsoil is permanently frozen.

TURBINE
A machine for producing continuous power in which a wheel or rotor is made to revolve often by a fast-moving flow of water.

UNITED NATIONS
An association of countries from around the world set up to prevent war and promote international co-operation.

URBANISATION
A population shift from rural to urban areas.

WATER BUTT
A large barrel or tank used for catching and storing rainwater.

WATER TABLE
The level to which the ground is saturated with water.

WATER VAPOUR
Water in gas form that is produced by evaporation or when water is heated.

INDEX

PICTURE CREDITS

The publisher would like to thank the following for their kind permission to reproduce their photographs:
Cover: Nadeem Zulfiqar/Dreamstime.com, Vladislav Gajic/Dreamstime.com; 2–3 Diianadimitrova/Dreamstime.com, 3b Gemenacom/Dreamstime.com, 3t Oleksandr Sokolenko/Dreamstime.com, 3c Welcomia/Dreamstime.com, 3b Photographerlondon/Dreamstime.com; 4 Whitthayap/Dreamstime.com; 5c Sjors737/Dreamstime.com, 5tr Samrat35/Dreamstime.com, 5b Compuinfoto/Dreamstime.com; 6–7 Roman Shyshak/Dreamstime.com; 8 Erectus/Dreamstime.com; 10–11 Jensphotos/Dreamstime.com, 11tr Gemenacom/Dreamstime.com; 12 Tr3gi/Dreamstime.com, 13 Samrat35/Dreamstime.com; 14–15 Irabel8/Dreamstime.com, 14b Asafta/Dreamstime.com; 16–17 Sjors737/Dreamstime.com, 19 Beijing Hetuchuangyi/Dreamstime.com; 20–21 Diianadimitrova/Dreamstime.com, 20b NASA, 21t Patrice Correia/Dreamstime.com, 21cr NASA; 22–23 Chase Dekker/Dreamstime.com, 23 Compuinfoto/Dreamstime.com; 26 Edwardje/Dreamstime.com, 27 Rainer Klotz/Dreamstime.com; 28 Oleksandr Sokolenko/Dreamstime.com, 29t Lighttouch/Dreamstime.com; 30bl NASA, 30br NASA, 31 NASA, 32–33 Vladimir Borodin/Dreamstime.com, 32 b Welcomia/Dreamstime.com, 33t Tulipmix/Dreamstime.com; 34c Kobby Dagan/Dreamstime.com, 34b Shawn Hempel/Dreamstime.com, 35 Moreno Soppelsa/Dreamstime.com, 36–37 Aschwin Prein/Dreamstime.com; 38–39 Alan Crosthwaite/Dreamstime.com; 40b Alamy.com, 41 Pikoli/Dreamstime.com; 42–43 Photographerlondon/Dreamstime.com; 44–45 Imkenneth/Dreamstime.com